EDGWARE

D0358151

COPY Ch.

Titles in Teen Reads:

Copy Cat	**Fair Game**	**Mama Barkfingers**
TOMMY DONBAVAND	ALAN DURANT	CAVAN SCOTT
Dead Scared	**Jigsaw Lady**	**Pest Control**
TOMMY DONBAVAND	TONY LEE	CAVAN SCOTT
Just Bite	**Mister Scratch**	**The Hunted**
TOMMY DONBAVAND	TONY LEE	CAVAN SCOTT
Home	**Stalker**	**The Changeling**
TOMMY DONBAVAND	TONY LEE	CAVAN SCOTT
Kidnap	**Dawn of the Daves**	**Nightmare**
TOMMY DONBAVAND	TIM COLLINS	ANN EVANS
Ward 13	**Joke Shop**	**Sitting Target**
TOMMY DONBAVAND	TIM COLLINS	JOHN TOWNSEND
Deadly Mission	**The Locals**	**Snow White, Black Heart**
MARK WRIGHT	TIM COLLINS	JACQUELINE RAYNER
Ghost Bell	**Troll**	**The Wishing Doll**
MARK WRIGHT	TIM COLLINS	BEVERLY SANFORD
The Corridor	**Insectoids**	**Underworld**
MARK WRIGHT	ROGER HURN	SIMON CHESHIRE
Death Road	**Billy Button**	**World Without Words**
JON MAYHEW	CAVAN SCOTT	JONNY ZUCKER

Badger Publishing Limited, Oldmedow Road, Hardwick Industrial Estate, King's Lynn PE30 4JJ
Telephone: 01438 791037

www.badgerlearning.co.uk

COPY CAT

TOMMY DONBAVAND

Copy Cat ISBN 978-1-78147-953-7

Text © Tommy Donbavand 2014
Complete work © Badger Publishing Limited 2014

Publisher: Susan Ross
Senior Editor: Danny Pearson
Publishing Assistant: Claire Morgan
Copyeditor: Cheryl Lanyon
Designer: Bigtop Design Ltd

2 4 6 8 10 9 7 5 3 1

CHAPTER 1

EMERGENCY

Sirens blared as two ambulances pulled into the hospital's emergency bay at exactly the same time. Identically dressed paramedics leaped out and opened the back doors to the vehicles as doctors and nurses came running to help.

Two wheeled stretchers were unloaded, each carrying the bloodied, unconscious figure of a teenage girl with short, reddish-brown hair...

CHAPTER 2

FRIENDS

Catherine Willows is weird. I feel really mean saying that – especially as I'm not exactly one of the cool kids myself – but it's true.

She's only been at our school for two weeks, and she's already attracted a lot of attention to herself. The wrong kind of attention, if you know what I mean. The kind of attention that gets you picked on.

For a start – she skips everywhere. And I mean everywhere! From class to class, in the playground – I even caught her skipping from one of the toilet cubicles to the sink to wash her hands.

She dresses in a strange way, too. We all have to wear uniform at our school and it's pretty dull. Black trousers or skirt, white shirt, black blazer and school tie. We look like a bunch of depressed clones shuffling along the corridors from room to room. But not Catherine...

She's covered the lapels of her blazer in metal badges with slogans like 'I can do it!', 'The best I can be!', and 'Top of the Class!'. Add to that the frilly collar of her shirt, the pink bobbles at the back of her socks and her blonde hair in bunches, and you can see why she stands out from the crowd.

"I feel sorry for her," I said to my best friend, Fiona, one lunch time.

"Sorry?" said Fiona, spitting out a lump of potato. "For weirdie Willows?"

"Yeah," I said, cleaning my glasses and putting them back on to look over at her. "She always sits by herself at lunch time."

"A lot of that is down to her Hello Kitty lunch box and My Little Pony backpack," said Fiona. "She should start acting her age instead of her shoe size."

I sighed and turned back to my plate of barely identifiable school dinner. "I know she doesn't exactly help herself," I said, running my fork through the thin, brown water that passed as gravy. "But maybe we could?"

"Could what?" asked Fiona, pushing her tray away, meal unfinished.

"I dunno… give her a makeover, perhaps? Teach her not to make so much of a target of herself all the time."

"Bit late for that," said Fiona, nodding to the other side of the room. I turned to see the biggest and meanest girl in our year – Minty Clinch – hauling Catherine up out of her seat.

"What did you just call me?" Minty roared.

"Nothing!" protested Catherine. "I didn't call you anything! I was just singing."

"And what were you singing?"

"'Puff, The Magic Dragon'," said Catherine.

I sighed. This wasn't going to get any better.

"You fink I look like a dragon, do ya?" bellowed Minty.

"N-no!" Catherine squeaked. "I just like the song and I was…"

Despite Fiona's protests, I raced across the dining room as quickly as I could. "Leave her alone, Minty!" I demanded.

The bully glared down at me, Catherine's collar still grasped in her fleshy fist. She'd drawn LOVE and HATE tattoos on her knuckles with blue ballpoint pen, but had misspelled HATE so that it read HATS.

"Or what, four eyes?" she growled. "What are you gonna do if I don't leave her alone?"

I shrugged. "I'll call a teacher."

Minty sniffed noisily then looked over my head to the rest of the silent dining room. Everyone was watching her closely.

"Never let me hear you singing that stupid song again!" she snarled, pushing Catherine back into her seat. Then she turned and marched out of the room, making a point of kicking as many chairs as possible on the way.

"Are you OK?" I asked Catherine.

"Yes, thank you," she nodded. "I really was only singing a song. I don't know what that large girl got so upset about."

"Don't worry about her," I said. "She just gets grumpy if she hasn't had enough raw meat for breakfast." I took a deep breath and resisted the urge to glance over at Fiona. I knew exactly what expression she'd have on her face. "Look, why don't you come over and sit with us to finish your lunch?"

Catherine literally trembled with excitement, making all her lapel badges jingle. "Really? Truly?"

"Yes, of course," I said, trying not to regret my decision already. "I'll help you carry your stuff."

So I picked up her tub of sandwiches with the crusts cut off and her packet of rainbow-drops and led the way back to our table. Catherine gathered together the rest of her belongings and skipped after me.

Fiona was looking at me like I'd just taken a dump in her favourite pair of shoes. "This is Catherine," I said as we sat down. "I'm Stacey and this is Fiona."

"Oh, call me Cat!" beamed Catherine.

"Everyone does. And by everyone, I mean you two – my new best friends!" She burst into a fit of laughter, punctuated by loud, rasping snorts.

Fiona stamped on my toes under the table.

"Did you see how brave Stacey was, standing up to that bully?" exclaimed Cat once she'd stopped giggle-grunting. "I expect she thought that awful girl wouldn't hit someone wearing glasses – especially ones as thick as those…"

And with that, she snatched my glasses off my face and put them on herself.

"Hey!" cried Fiona, reaching out. "Give those back to her!"

"Gosh!" said Cat, peering through my lenses. "You must have really terrible eyes to need glasses like these!"

I squinted at the blurred shape sitting beside me. "I do have bad eyes," I said. "It's a kind of degenerative illness called Stargardt Syndrome."

Cat laughed and punched me in the arm. "You just made that up, silly!"

I couldn't see Fiona clearly, but her sigh of frustration told me exactly what she was thinking.

"I wish I had made it up," I said politely. "But it runs in the family. Both my mum and dad have lost most of their sight because of it already."

Cat gasped. "So you're going to go blind from it?"

I nodded. "It certainly looks that way…"

Cat whipped off my glasses as if they were suddenly diseased and tossed them onto the table in front of me, one of the lenses plopping into my unfinished pool of gravy.

By the time I'd cleaned them and put them back on, Cat was rooting deep in her My Little Pony backpack. "Well, we can still be friends until that happens," she promised. "Now – who wants a Barbie fun bracelet?"

CHAPTER 3

HAIR

I didn't see Cat for a few days after that. Not because I was avoiding her – really! We just didn't have the same classes for the last part of the week.

Fiona was still unhappy about the way she had treated me. "She practically called you a freak!" she said as we got changed after PE.

"No she didn't," I insisted. "She was just, I dunno… not very tactful about my eye problem. That's all."

"Not very tactful?" cried Fiona. "She was terrified she was going to catch blindness from you!"

I chuckled. "She wouldn't even take a piece of chewing gum from me on the way back to class."

"Good thing, too!" Fiona giggled. "Classic way of spreading eye problems, sharing an unprotected packet of chewing gum."

We laughed as we continued to get changed, but the truth was, Cat had hurt my feelings a little bit when she'd asked about my eye problems. I know she hadn't meant it that way, and I've long since got over people calling me names like 'specky' and 'goggle eyes'; but the fact that she'd seemed afraid of my illness – I'd never had that before.

"What are you doing tonight?" asked Fiona as she buttoned up her shirt. "Fancy coming round and watching a DVD? We could get a pizza…"

"Can't, sorry," I said. "Arjun's coming round for tea."

Fiona's eyes grew wide. "Oooh! Introducing the parents to your boyfriend at long last!"

I pushed her away, my cheeks burning. "Arjun's *not* my boyfriend!" I protested. "He's just a friend…"

"A friend that you held hands with in the cinema last week!" teased Fiona. "I'm hurt, Stacey! You've never held my hand when we went to see a movie!"

"That's because you're not as good looking as Arjun!" I said, swinging my bag over my shoulder and heading for the changing-room exit.

Fiona and I laughed as we walked through the woods at the back of the school on our way home.

*

I waited nervously outside the 24-hour shop on the corner of our street, feeling completely overdressed in a skirt and top. Usually I'm in a tracksuit or even my pyjamas by this time of the evening.

I checked my watch for the thirtieth time in five minutes. Arjun was late. He'd said he'd meet me here at –

"You look nice!"

I spun round to find Arjun standing behind me. He'd come from the other end of the street – and he was clutching a bunch of flowers.

Then he kissed me on the cheek!

"Thanks!" I said. "So do you... look nice, I mean!" What was I prattling on about? I hadn't even looked at what he was wearing! I felt like such an idiot. Come on – deep breath, Stacey. OK...

Then I noticed that Arjun was trembling. He was as nervous about this evening as I was! Somehow, that made me feel a lot better.

"Flowers!" I said, reaching for the bouquet – but Arjun pulled them away.

"They're for your mum," he said with a smile. "And your dad, if he likes flowers as well…"

"My mum loves flowers," I said, my heart finally slowing. "Especially ones that smell pretty. You might want to take the price off, though…"

It was Arjun's turn to blush. "Oops!" He tried to peel the label off and failed miserably. It tore in half, leaving a sticky mess behind.

"Give it here!" I smiled, trying to get my nails under the edge of the price tag.

"Gosh! Look at you two lovebirds!" said a voice.

I turned to see Cat skipping down the road towards us. "Oh, er… hello," I said. "What are you doing here? Do you live nearby?"

Cat shook her head. "My uncle's house is on the other side of town, near the motorway," she said. "I was coming to see you."

And then I noticed her hair. The blonde bunches had gone. She'd had it cut short and dyed a reddish-brown. Exactly the same as my hair!

"What have you done?" I asked, staring at her new style.

"Do you like it?" giggled Cat, twirling round. "I thought yours looked so lovely, I took a picture of it when you weren't looking and had mine done the same way! That's why I was coming round   to show you."

I frowned. "Hang on – how did you know where I lived?"

"Easy peasy, lemon squeezy!" she beamed. "I copied your address down from your school bus pass when you were doing PE."

"You went into my bag in the changing room!"
I exclaimed.

"I couldn't disturb you to ask; you were
playing hockey."

"Well, shouldn't you have been in lessons
as well?"

"I was," said Cat. "I saw you out on the hockey
field from Chemistry and pretended that I didn't
feel well so I could slip out."

I didn't know what to say. "I can't… It's just…"

"Calm down, Stacey," said Arjun, placing
a hand on my shoulder. "I'm sure it's just a
misunderstanding…"

"So is this your boyfriend?" asked Cat, gazing
up at Arjun. "He's a bit dishy, isn't he?" She
leaned into me and whispered loudly. "I know
you've got bad eyes and everything, but did you
know he's Pakistani?"

"Actually, I'm from Burnley," said Arjun. "But my parents are from India."

"It's OK," Cat said slowly and loudly to him. "Stacey's parents are almost blind, so they won't be able to tell you're dark skinned if you don't mention it."

"Right," I said through gritted teeth. "I think you'd better be leaving."

"But, I've only just got here," said Cat. "I used up all my money on the bus fare."

"Then how were you planning to get home?"

"I thought your dad could drive me back."

I fought to control my temper. "My dad doesn't drive," I said. "His eyesight…"

"Oh, yeah…" said Cat. "Well, maybe he could lend me the taxi fare instead."

"Arjun is coming round to my house for tea," I pointed out.

"Well, I won't be in the way," Cat smiled. "And I don't eat much. I'll just pick off your plate." She linked arms with both of us. "Come on, then…"

"Actually, I think I'll head home, if you don't mind," said Arjun, pulling away from Cat. "We'll do this another time." He handed me the bouquet with the torn price label. "Give these to your mum."

"We will!" Cat beamed.

Then Arjun was off, hurrying back the way he'd come.

"Never mind him," said Cat, cuddling into me. "It'll save you a lot of bother in the long run. Now, what's for tea?"

CHAPTER 4

BAG

"I'm Cat, and I'm really thrilled to meet you both," said Cat as she shook hands with my mum and dad. "Stacey's already told me about your eye syndrome thingy and how you gave it to her, so don't feel embarrassed. Fingers crossed you never have grandchildren or they'll get it, too."

She pushed her way past my parents and into the living room. "Oh, I love the way you've decorated!"

"I was expecting Stacey's friend, Arjun," said my mum, following quickly.

"He had to rush off," Cat smiled. "Probably prayer time at his mosque or something. You did know he was Pakistani, didn't you?"

I sighed. "Cat, he's not from – "

But Cat didn't show any sign of hearing me. "He got you these," she said, pressing the flowers into my mum's hand. He left the price on there but you won't be able to read it, so let's just pretend they were expensive, eh?"

"Would you, er… like a drink, Cat?" my dad asked.

Cat turned to me. "What are you having?"

"What? Oh, I don't know… probably a glass of Coke."

"Then I'll have the same," said Cat. "But don't let us girls stop you enjoying a drop of the hard stuff, Mr Green! No one would even notice if you were to get blind drunk, after all!"

Then she sniffed at the air and dashed into the kitchen. "What is that gorgeous smell?"

My mum and dad turned to look at me – and all I could do was shrug.

"It needs more salt!" shouted Cat.

*

"She stayed all evening?" said Fiona, aghast.

I nodded, yawning. "She left at twenty to midnight – after our third game of family Pictionary."

Fiona thought for a second. "But how can your mum and dad play Pictionary with their eyesight?"

"They can't," I said. "I suppose they didn't want to hurt her feelings. They just guessed at random objects until the time ran out."

"What a nightmare!"

"I know! And then, when I woke up this morning, I found a note from her under my pillow promising to be my best friend forever."

"She went into your room?"

I shrugged. "She must have. Probably when she went to the toilet."

"How did she get home?"

"My dad paid for her taxi," I said, "but here's the strange thing... she told me she lived with her uncle out near the motorway – but she wanted the taxi to go to her brother's flat in the town."

"Maybe her family have to share her to stop themselves from going loopy?" giggled Fiona.

Despite my tiredness, I laughed. "You might be right!"

Fiona and I were sitting in the snack bar of the DVD shop in the shopping centre, having our traditional milkshake before we hit the clothes boutiques. We didn't always buy stuff – certainly not at some of their prices – but we liked trying on different outfits and parading up and down in front of the dressing-room mirrors.

We were in the second clothes shop when Fiona spotted Cat. "Watch out!" she said. "Oddball at two o'clock…"

I looked up to see Cat browsing through the rails and felt an involuntary shudder run down my spine.

"You weren't wrong," hissed Fiona. "Her hair is just like yours!"

And that wasn't all… Cat was wearing exactly the same skirt and blouse I'd chosen for my family tea with Arjun the night before.

I couldn't help myself. I strode across the shop, grabbed her shoulder and spun her around. "Alright," I said. "What's your game?"

"Stacey!" cried Cat, kissing the air on either side of my cheeks. "Who knew I'd run into my bestie at the weekend?"

"What are you wearing?" I demanded.

Cat looked surprised at my tone. "What, this little outfit?" she said innocently. "Please don't judge me harshly – they were the first two things that fell out of my wardrobe this morning."

"But, I – "

"And please do thank your mum and dad for the wonderful time we had last night, even if the spaghetti bolognese did have too much garlic in it…"

"You certainly ate enough of it!"

"I didn't want to seem rude," said Cat. "It can't be easy for your mum to make dinner with her eyesight problems." She sniffed back a tear. "And it's not often I get a home-cooked meal, these days. Not with my uncle's problems…"

"I thought you lived with your brother," I said flatly.

"No," said Cat. "I just went there last night to check he was behaving himself. One more strike and he'll go to prison for good."

I scowled. "Prison?"

Cat nodded sadly. "It's not his fault, really," she said. "He's a single parent, just trying to care for his son. He didn't mean to steal that baby milk..."

How did she do it? How did she make me care every time?

Fiona came over to join us. "Cat..." she grunted.

"Hello, Fiona!" beamed Cat, suddenly happy again. "Are you going to spend the afternoon with Stacey and me?"

I blinked. "I'm spending the afternoon with you?"

"Well, you must have tracked me down for a reason," said Cat.

"No, wait… I didn't track you – "

Fiona's phone pinged as she received a text. She pulled it out to read the message.

"Ooh, I like your mobile!" said Cat, peering over her shoulder. "I wish I had one like that…"

Fiona pulled the phone tightly to her chest. "I've got to go," she said.

"Why?" I asked. "Is everything alright?"

"I've… just got to do something," Fiona replied. "I'll see you on Monday." Then she gathered up her bags and hurried out of the shop.

Cat wrapped her arms around me. "Looks like it's just the two of us, then!"

So I spent the afternoon window-shopping with Cat and, to be honest, it wasn't as bad as

I'd expected it to be. She did get very excited whenever I tried something on, and she always insisted on choosing a matching outfit for herself so we could 'see what we would look like if we were twins', but I got the impression this was the first time anyone had done anything like this with her.

Then she spotted a bag the same as mine in one of the department stores. "I have to have this!" she gasped, pulling a ball of silver foil from her pocket. "Keep watch for me!"

"Why?" I said, alarmed. "What are you going to do?"

Cat opened up the foil and wrapped it around the electronic security tag pinned to the handle of the bag. "The foil will stop the alarm from going off at the shop doorway," she said.

"What?"

"Don't worry!" Cat smiled. "I do this all the time. Just stay calm and no one will even look at us."

And with that, she marched towards the exit.

My mouth was suddenly dry. I couldn't let her do this. I gave chase and grabbed the bag just as she was going past one of the sensors. "Put that back!" I hissed, pulling hard.

"Let go!" Cat cried. "You'll attract attention to us!" It was true; people were starting to look in our direction.

"I don't care!" I shouted. "This is stealing!"

Then the foil slipped off the security tag and the alarm went off.

"Hey!" called a burly security guard, heading our way.

"Run!" yelled Cat, racing out of the shop with the bag.

I don't know why, but I ran, too.

The security guard chased us along the upper

mall of the shopping centre. Cat dodged in and out of the crowds nimbly. I tried to keep up with her, tears stinging my eyes as I bumped into shopper after shopper. Why was I doing this? Why didn't I just stop and try to explain things?

Eventually, the guard stopped, out of breath. I found Cat in the corridor outside the toilets, removing the security tag with a small pair of pliers.

"There!" she said, tossing the broken tag into a nearby bin and swinging the bag over her shoulder. "Now we really look like twins."

"What the hell do you think you're doing?" I demanded.

Cat shrugged. "It's a nice bag."

"It's stealing!" I protested, keeping my voice down as a young mother and her daughter came out of the toilets.

"What do you want to do next?" said Cat. "I fancy a coffee…"

"You're mad!" I said. "Everyone at school is right. You're mad! I gave you a chance because I felt sorry for you, but no more. I'm not staying here with you one second longer."

I turned and started to walk away, but Cat called after me, "I'll tell you where Fiona has gone…"

CHAPTER 5

GLASSES

I hammered on the door, not letting up. After a while, Fiona's mum appeared in her dressing gown.

"Stacey..." she said, blinking in the early morning light. "Do you know what time it is?"

"I'm sorry," I said. "But Fiona didn't answer her phone all last night, or this morning, and I need to talk to her. Is she in her room?"

I didn't wait for an answer. I pushed past Fiona's mum and took the stairs two at a time. I paused for a second at the bedroom door, then charged in. Fiona was still in bed.

"Why?" I demanded, pulling her duvet off her. "Why him?"

Fiona tried to drag the duvet back from me, but I held it tight. "I don't know what you're talking about…"

"You don't?" I snapped. "Then let me give you a few clues – popcorn, large Cokes, a romantic comedy, holding hands, KISSING!"

Fiona shrank back on her bed. "You saw us?"

"Yes, I saw you!" I shouted. "Cat read his text over your shoulder. You left me with her to go on a date with Arjun!"

"You… you weren't meant to know…"

I sank to the floor, sobbing. "You don't understand, do you? I'm not like you. You're pretty. I've got these…" I pulled off my glasses. "Boys aren't interested in girls like me – and then Arjun came along. I couldn't believe it. Couldn't believe that he wanted to spend time with someone like me."

Fiona was crying as well now. "I'm sorry," she said through her tears. "I didn't mean it to happen."

I almost laughed. "So it was all an accident? You just happened to go to the cinema by yourself and fell on his face?"

"He sent me a note," Fiona explained.

I wiped my eyes. "A note? What kind of note?"

"You don't want to know," said Fiona. "Forget I mentioned it."

"What note?"

With a sigh, Fiona slid open the drawer in her bedside table and pulled out a slip of paper. I took it from her and read the words inside. It was from Arjun, saying that he'd only been spending time with me because he didn't have the courage to ask out the girl he was really interested in – Fiona.

"I'm sorry, Stacey!" Fiona blubbed.

I barely heard her. My hands were shaking and the blood was pounding in my ears. I'd seen that handwriting before – on a note left under my pillow at home.

It was Cat's handwriting.

*

I had to wait until after Maths the following morning before I could confront Cat. I'd sat patiently all the way through the lesson, planning what I was going to say to her. She sat at the front, happily answering the teacher's questions as though there was nothing wrong in the world.

She was dressed differently, too. Gone were the lapel badges and the frilly blouse. She was wearing a standard school uniform, which made her look more like me than ever before.

Then the bell rang...

I pinned her up against the wall as soon as she left the classroom. "Why did you do it?" I demanded.

"Gosh, Stacey!" Cat exclaimed. "What on earth has come over you?"

"Shut it!" I snarled. "You sent Fiona that note!"

"Yes, I did," Cat admitted. "Still, they make a cute couple, don't they? Just call me the matchmaker..."

"Arjun was *my* boyfriend!"

"Really?" said Cat. "I heard you tell Fiona that you were just friends, so I thought it would be fine to get those two lovebirds together."

Suddenly, a fleshy hand covered in blue ballpoint pen clamped down on my shoulder. "Oi! What do you fink you're doing?"

"It's OK, Minty," said Cat with a smile. "It's just a little misunderstanding."

"Doesn't look like that to me," said Minty. "Stacey looks like she's going to fump ya!"

"No," beamed Cat. "Stacey wouldn't hit anyone wearing glasses…" Then she reached into her blazer and pulled out a pair of spectacles that were identical to mine and slipped them on.

I released my grip and stumbled back a step. "What…?"

"It took a while to find the same frames," Cat said. "And the lenses are just clear glass, of course; I don't have your silly degenerative eye problem. But I think they suit me!"

I felt the corridor spin around me. I had to get out of there. "You're crazy," I croaked, staggering away. The bell rang for the start of the next lesson, but I needed some fresh air.

I burst out through the doors and into the playground. I'd never missed a class before. If anyone caught me, I'd be in a lot of trouble – but I didn't care. I had to get things straight in my head. I started to run, making for the area of woodland at the back of the school.

Once I was out of sight of the classrooms, I slumped back against a tree and took a deep breath. I've always liked these woods; Fiona and I often walked through them on the way home, even though it makes the journey a little longer.

My mind was racing. Fiona… my best friend, or at least she was. Now she was going out with Arjun. No, she'd been tricked into going out with him. Although he'd gone along with it all without complaining. I guess I was wrong about him from the start. He'd always seemed so –

A lightning bolt of pain shot through my head and I crumpled to the ground, my glasses falling somewhere. Blinking hard, I tentatively touched the back of my head. My fingers came away covered with blood.

Scared, I fumbled for my glasses, my vision more blurred than usual. Finally, my fingers found them and I slipped them back on. One of the lenses was cracked, but at least I could see again…

I heard movement and spun round, still on my knees. Cat was standing over me, a large rock clutched in her hands. She'd hit me!

"You've got it all," she said, flatly. "Everything I've never had."

She brought the rock down again. I scuttled back, but couldn't get completely out of the way. The stone hit my knee, and I heard the bone CRACK as I cried out.

"Stop this, please!" I begged, pushing myself further away from Cat.

"I can't," said Cat. "It's almost finished…"

"What is?" I asked, my voice trembling.

"My plan, silly!" smiled Cat. "My plan to take your place…"

"T-take my place?"

"Of course!" Cat beamed, raising the rock over her head again. "You go away, and I get to be Stacey."

I didn't want to think about what she meant by 'go away'. "But people will know," I said, pushing further away from her. My knee was agony, and I felt my vision begin to close in. No! I couldn't allow myself to pass out…

Cat swung the rock down again, this time missing my ear by centimetres and smashing into my shoulder. I screamed.

"I look just like you now, you see," she said. "Your mum and dad can't see properly – they'll just think I'm you."

I pressed down on the ground to shuffle back further, but my shoulder gave way and I collapsed. Cat grinned and hefted the rock once more.

"There are other people…" I gasped. "Fiona… teachers at school…"

"I've thought it all through!" said Cat confidently. "I'll tell mum and dad – my mum and dad – that I've fallen out with Fiona and I want to swap to another school. A fresh start in a new uniform – as Stacey Green!"

My ears were ringing as unconsciousness crept closer. "But… your family… your uncle… brother…"

"I made them up!" giggled Cat. "Fooled you, too! There's only me, no one else. They can't even keep me in one of those stupid care homes for long. I always find a way out. But, this time, I never need to go back. Not now I'm Stacey Green!"

"No!" I groaned, wincing with pain. "I'm Stacey Green!"

"Well, we can't both be Stacey Green, silly!" Cat cackled. "So we have to choose which one of us will get out of here alive…"

She began to swing the rock down one final time. I lashed out with my good leg and kicked her hard in the stomach. Cat grunted and doubled over, the rock falling harmlessly to the ground. She reached for it, but I kicked out again, this time catching her in the face, breaking her version of my glasses. I heard her nose break along with the plastic frames.

"Only one Stacey Green gets out alive?" I said. "Fine by me!"

We glared at each other through the broken lenses of our glasses for a second, then we both lunged for the blood-stained rock.

CHAPTER 6

SURVIVOR

The nurse looked up as the teenage girl's bed was wheeled into the side room, a consultant surgeon close behind.

"She made it through surgery, then?" said the nurse as she connected the girl up to the waiting machinery.

The surgeon nodded. "It was touch and go for a while — her injuries are pretty bad — but she should pull through."

"And the other girl? The one that came in with her?"

"I'm afraid not," the surgeon replied.

The pair worked silently for a moment.

"I wonder what it was all about," the nurse said eventually. "Why two school friends would attack each other in such a horrific way?"

"We'll have to wait until she wakes up before she can tell us that," said the surgeon. "Whoever she is…"

"Oh, we know her name now…" said the nurse. "The blood test results came back. Both girls had been here when they were younger, so we had them on record."

"That's something," said the surgeon. "He plucked a clipboard from the end of the bed and took a pen from his shirt pocket. "Go on, nurse, who is she?"

The nurse double-checked her notes, then looked down at the unconscious girl in the bed. "Her name is…"

THE END